D1413838

This book belongs to

....

Original poem by Clement Clarke Moore.
Illustrated by Clare Fennell.

'Twas the Night Before Christmas

Clement Clarke Moore

•

Clare Fennell

make
believe
ideas

'Twas the night before Christmas, when all through the house
not a creature was stirring, not even a mouse.
The stockings were hung by the chimney with care,
in hopes that St. Nicholas soon would be there.

The children were nestled all **snug** in their beds,
while visions of **sugarplums** danced in their heads.

And **Mama** in her 'kerchief, and I in my cap,
had just settled our brains for a **long winter's** nap.

When out on the lawn there arose such a clatter,
I sprang from the bed to see what was the matter.
Away to the window

I flew like a flash,

tore open

the shutters, and

threw up

the sash.

The moon, on the breast of the new-fallen snow,
gave the luster of mid-day to objects below.

When, what to my wondering
eyes should appear . . .

. . . but a miniature sleigh and eight tiny reindeer,

with a little old driver, so lively and quick,

I knew in a moment it must be St. Nick.

More rapid than eagles his coursers they came,

and he whistled, and shouted,

and called them by name.

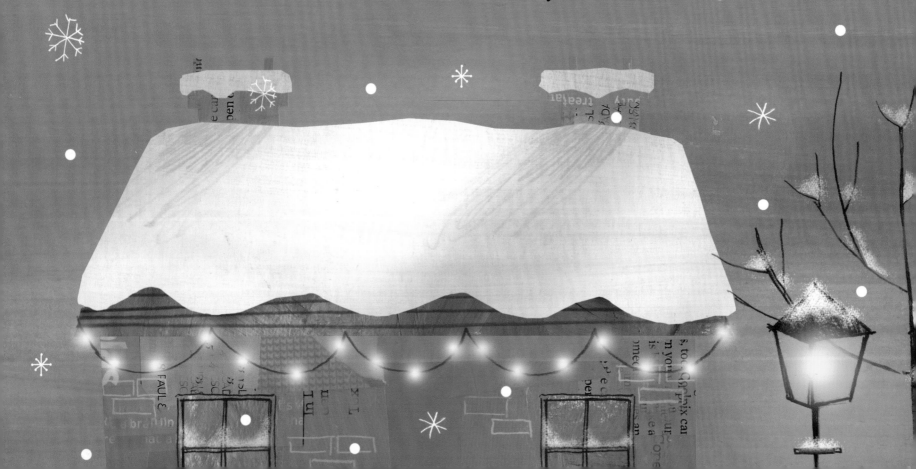

On, **Comet!** On, *Cupid!*
On, *Donner* and Blitzen!

To the top of the porch! To the top of the wall!
Now, *dash* away! Dash away! *Dash* away all!"

As dry leaves that before the *wild* hurricane fly,

when they meet with an obstacle, mount to the sky;

so up to the housetop the coursers they *flew*,

with the sleigh full of *toys*, and St. Nicholas, too.

And then, in a *twinkling*, I heard on the roof
the **prancing** and *pawing* of each little hoof.

As I **drew** in my head, and was turning around,
down the chimney St. Nicholas came with a **bound.**

He was dressed all in fur,
from his head to his foot,
and his clothes were all tarnished
with ashes and soot.

A bundle of toys
was flung on his back,
and he looked like a peddler
just opening his pack.

His eyes – how they *twinkled!* His dimples – how **merry!**

His **cheeks** were like *roses*, his nose like a **cherry!**

His **droll** little mouth was drawn up like a *bow*,

and the **beard** on his chin was as white as the *snow*.

The **stump** of a pipe he held **tight** in his teeth,

and the *smoke*, it encircled his head like a **wreath**.

He had a **broad** face and a little round *belly*
that sh**oo**k when he *laughed*, like a bowlful of jelly!
He was **chubby** and *plump*, a right jolly old *elf*,
and I **laughed** when I saw him, in spite of myself.

A **wink** of his eye and a **twist** of his head

soon gave me to know I had **nothing** to dread.

He spoke **not** a word,

but went **straight** to his work,

and **filled** all the *stockings*;

then turned

with a jerk,

and laying his finger

aside of his nose,

and giving a nod,

up the

chimney

he rose!

He sprang to his **sleigh**, to his team gave a *whistle*,
and away they all **flew**, like the down of a **thistle**.

But I heard him **exclaim**, as he drove out of sight,

"**Happy Christmas** to all,

and to **all** a *good night!*"